What's the Matter with
CARRUTHERS?

A Bedtime Story

written and illustrated by

JAMES MARSHALL

HOUGHTON MIFFLIN COMPANY BOSTON

Printed in the United States of America

RNF   ISBN   0-395-13895-7
PAP   ISBN   0-395-45358-5

Y   10   9   8   7   6   5

To

Susan Korn

and

Harry Allard

One fall morning Emily Pig and her friend Eugene were taking a stroll in the park.

"What beautiful weather," said Emily. "I'm sure we are going to meet some of our friends here today."

"That would be very nice indeed," said Eugene. "It's such fun to bump into friends and have a little chat."

And sure enough, just around the bend, they came upon their old friend Carruthers, all bundled up in his muffler and sitting alone on a wooden bench. He was gazing at the falling leaves.

"Good morning, Carruthers," they called out in their most cheerful voices.

"Good morning," said Carruthers. But his voice was far from cheerful. It was the kind of "good morning" that really means, "Don't bother me. I want to be left alone."

"I'm worried about Carruthers," whispered Emily to Eugene. "He hasn't been himself lately. He's so grumpy and unpleasant."

"It's not like Carruthers to be unpleasant," Eugene whispered back. "He always has a kind word for everyone."

"Yesterday," said Emily, "I saw him do such a disgraceful thing. You may find this hard to believe, but Carruthers actually stuck out his tongue at someone!"

Eugene was shocked. "It's not like Carruthers to be rude. He has always had such lovely manners."

"But that's not all," said Emily. "The children in the park are complaining. It seems that Carruthers took away their ball."

"Oh, no!" exclaimed Eugene. "I just can't understand it. It is certainly not like Carruthers to be mean. He has always been so fond of children."

Leaving Carruthers to sit alone on his bench and gaze at the falling leaves, Emily and Eugene continued their stroll through the park.

"There must be something that we can do to lift Carruthers' spirits," said Emily. "And we had better do it soon. If Carruthers continues to act the way he has been acting, he won't have any friends left."

"That's very true," said Eugene. "No one likes a grouch."

And so the two friends sat together on a large rock and thought long and hard.

"Well," Eugene began, after a long pause, "whenever I'm in a grouchy and unpleasant mood, I always listen to beautiful music. In no time at all I feel much better, and I'm sure that I'm much more pleasant to be around."

"That gives me an idea," said Emily. "Come with me."

The two friends hurried home, but in a few minutes, they were back in the park with their musical instruments. Emily was carrying her tuba, and Eugene had his tambourine.

"What a good idea," said Eugene. "When we smooth Carruthers' rumpled nerves with our beautiful music, he'll be his old friendly self again. I'm sure that he'll be so grateful."

Turning the bend, they saw Carruthers, still sitting in the same place, still gazing at the falling leaves. And ever so quietly they tiptoed up behind him.

Placing the mouthpiece of her tuba to her lips, Emily puffed up her cheeks and began to play, softly at first and then quite loudly. Eugene tapped on his tambourine.

"Um-Pah Um-Pah Tap Tap. Um-Pah Um-Pah Tap Tap." It sounded something like that.

But Carruthers was not impressed. Instead of listening to the music, he put his paws to his ears and growled, "That is the most awful noise I have ever heard in my life!"

And he promptly got up and walked away.

Emily Pig and Eugene looked at each other. "Maybe we should have practiced more," said Eugene.

"No," replied his friend, "some bears just don't and never will appreciate good music."

Emily set her tuba on the bench and sat down beside it. "But just because we could not improve Carruthers' mood with our music, that does not mean that we should give up. We must think of another way."

"Yes," replied Eugene, "we must not give up."

So once again they thought long and hard.

"Whenever I am in a grumpy mood," said Emily, "I always have a little snack. I'm sure that a tasty snack would be just the thing for Carruthers. Maybe he hasn't been getting enough to eat lately. Why don't we invite him to lunch for honey cakes and tea? You know how partial bears are to honey cakes."

"What a clever idea," said Eugene. "Let's go to your house right away and send Carruthers an invitation to come to lunch."

Carruthers was in an even grouchier mood when he came home from the park and found the invitation to

lunch waiting for him. Certainly he was in no mood to go
visiting — but what bear can resist honey cakes? So of
course he went.

At Emily's house Carruthers was given the very best
chair. Emily poured the tea and Eugene brought out the
honey cakes.

"It's another beautiful day, isn't it?" said Emily, trying to start a friendly conversation.

"Not really," said Carruthers.

"You must enjoy strolling in the park," said Eugene.

"Not especially," said Carruthers.

"My, how lovely your fur looks today, Carruthers," said Emily.

"I've never cared for it," said Carruthers.

Emily and Eugene didn't know what else to say, Car-

ruthers was so determined to be unpleasant. And so the tea party continued in silence, except for the sound of Carruthers munching on honey cakes and sipping tea.

When the cake plate and the teapot were both empty, Eugene tried again. "My goodness, Carruthers, you certainly must like Emily's honey cakes. You've eaten all twelve dozen of them."

"They were very tasty," said Carruthers. "Thank you for inviting me, but I must leave now. Stuffy in here."

"Yes, it is stuffy," said Emily. "Why don't we all go for a walk in the fresh air?"

"I don't like walking," said Carruthers.

"Then why don't we all go for a drive?" said Eugene.

"A splendid idea!" exclaimed Emily. "I'm sure a change of scene will do wonders for Carruthers."

And before Carruthers could say anything at all, he found himself all bundled up again and sitting in the back seat of Emily's traveling car.

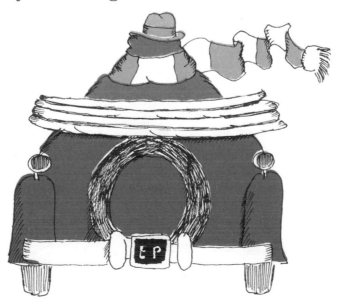

Very soon the three friends were sailing through the open countryside.

"There's nothing like a drive in the country to cheer the spirits," called out Eugene.

"The countryside gives me hay fever," was all Carruthers would say.

Not far down the road they passed a large sign.

"Ah," said Emily.

"Ah," said Eugene.

"Ugh," said Carruthers, "I hate amusement parks."

But Emily and Eugene paid no attention, no attention at all. "Rides and games are just what Carruthers needs," whispered Eugene.

"Yes," said Emily. "We are going, and that is that."

When they got to the park Carruthers asked to stay in the car, but Emily would have none of that. "Nonsense, Carruthers, you must not be a bad sport."

Carruthers had never been very good at arguing, especially with Emily, and so he went in to the amusement park. And he rode all the rides and played all the games that Emily told him to play.

But nothing seemed to improve his mood. He didn't smile even once. Not even on the ferris wheel, which had always been his favorite ride. He grumbled all through the fun house and looked distinctly annoyed in the tunnel of love. And even after Carruthers had won several lovely prizes, he was still the grouch he had been all day. "I think it's time to go home. I'm not having a good time."

Emily and Eugene were so discouraged. "I was sure this would work," said Emily. "It seems to me that we have tried just about everything, and Carruthers hasn't improved one little bit."

"Yes," said Eugene, "I suppose there is nothing to do but take Carruthers home."

On the way home no one spoke.

But when the roadster pulled up in front of Carruthers' little house, Emily had one last idea. "Carruthers," she said, "just look at all those leaves in your front yard. What a messy housekeeper you are. I really think we should help you rake some of them up before evening."

Now this was an idea that Carruthers did not like at all. Raking leaves in the late afternoon was not exactly his notion of fun, but he knew that Emily was going to have her way again. And he went off to find three rakes and a bushel basket.

"I don't see why we should help Carruthers rake his leaves," said Eugene to Emily, "after all we have done for him today."

But Emily had made up her mind. "Sometimes keeping very busy is a good way to get out of a grumpy mood," she explained.

"We might as well give it a try," sighed Eugene.

When Carruthers returned, the three leaf-rakers set to work. Emily and Carruthers raked leaves into the bushel basket, and Eugene emptied the contents onto a pile he had started.

Very soon the pile was quite high.

"If we hurry," said Emily, "we will be finished in time
for supper."

But Carruthers was already beginning to slow down.

He started to yawn. A small yawn, which he covered

with his paw, to be polite.

Then a much bigger yawn.

But then—a great big bear yawn.

And without a word of warning, Carruthers plopped
headfirst into the huge pile of leaves.

"Oh my goodness!" cried Eugene. "What in the world
has happened?"

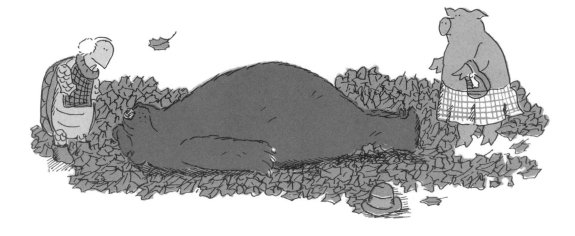

The two friends quickly cleared away the pile of leaves and uncovered Carruthers.

"He's asleep!" they exclaimed.

"So that is why Carruthers has been such an awful grouch lately," said Emily. "Why didn't we think of this before? He forgot that it was time for his long winter's sleep."

"Of course," said Eugene. "Carruthers should have been tucked away in bed several days ago. No wonder he has been so impossible to be around."

"There is no use waking him now," said Emily. "He'll be asleep for the rest of the winter. It's up to us to get him into bed."

"That will be the hardest job yet," said Eugene.

But after a lot of huffing and puffing they managed to lift the sleeping Carruthers, who was just beginning to snore, into a small wagon and pull it into the house.

When they got to Carruthers' bedroom, they huffed and puffed again and ever so slowly put Carruthers under the heavy winter covers. Emily pulled his nightcap snugly down around his ears. Eugene set the alarm clock for spring and drew the shades.

"Good night, Carruthers," whispered Emily, giving him a kiss on the cheek. "Sleep tight, and we'll see you in the spring when you will be your old sweet self again."